The Taxi That Hurried

REISSUED ON THE OCCASION OF
THE 50TH ANNIVERSARY OF LITTLE GOLDEN BOOKS

By Lucy Sprague Mitchell,
Irma Simonton Black, and Jessie Stanton

Pictures by Tibor Gergely

A GOLDEN BOOK • NEW YORK
Western Publishing Company, Inc.,
Racine, Wisconsin 53404

ONCE there was a taxi. It was a bright yellow taxi with two red lines running around its body. Inside it had a soft leather seat and two hard little let-down seats.

It was a smart little taxi. For it could start fast—jerk-whizz!! It could tear along the street—whizz-squeak!! It could stop fast—squeak-jerk!!

Its driver's name was Bill. Together they were a speedy pair.

One day the taxi was standing on the street close to the sidewalk. Bill and the little taxi didn't like to stand still long. "I wonder who will be our next passengers," thought Bill.

Just then Bill heard some feet running on
the sidewalk, thump, thump, thump! And he
heard some smaller feet pattering along, too,
thumpety, thumpety, thumpety!

He leaned out and saw Tom with a little suitcase and Tom's mother with a big suitcase. And both of them were breathing hard.

"Oh!" gasped Tom's mother. "Taxi-driver man, please drive us to the station as fast as you can. We're very late and the train won't wait. Oh!—oh!—oh!"

Tom and his mother tumbled into the taxi and slammed the door.

"Sure, lady," answered Bill. "We're a speedy pair. We can get you there."

Away went the taxi like a yellow streak.

Tom and his mother bounced and jounced on the leather seats. Then suddenly, squeak-jerk! The taxi stopped short. Ahead shone a red light. Underneath the light stood a big traffic policeman.

Tom's mother called, "Taxi-driver man, must you stop when lights are red? We simply have to get ahead. We're *terribly* late and the train won't wait."

And Bill answered, "Surely, lady, you have seen how cars must wait till lights are green. But we're a speedy pair, we'll surely get you there." Then suddenly, jerk-whizz! They were off again down the crowded street.

For the light had changed to green again.

Away went the taxi down the street faster than ever. Now it had to turn and twist, for the street was full of traffic—trucks and wagons and other taxis. The little taxi hurried past them all like a yellow streak and people could hardly see Tom's little face looking out of the window as he bounced and jounced by. "My!" said the people on the sidewalk. "That's a speedy taxi. I wonder why it's in such a hurry. Lucky it's got such a good driver." The taxi wiggled around a big bus. It jiggled across a trolley track. Then suddenly, squeak-jerk! The little taxi stopped short again.

It stood stock still behind a big coal truck that was backing up to the sidewalk. For the driver was trying hard to get his truck just the right way for the black coal to go jumping and clattering down its slide into a hole in the sidewalk.

Tom stood up so that he could see the big coal truck better. He could see the handle on the side. He wished he could watch the driver turn that handle and make the big truck tip up in front. He almost wished they were not in such a hurry.

Tom's mother called, "Taxi-driver man, first it's a cop that makes you stop and now we're stuck behind a truck. We're *awfully* late and the train won't wait."

So Bill called to the truck driver, "Please, will you try to let me get by?"

And the truck driver grinned and stopped his truck. Carefully and slowly Bill squeezed by the big coal truck, close to the sidewalk.

Bill called over his shoulder, "We're a speedy pair. We'll get you there."

Tom's mother bounced so hard on the wide leather seat that her head whacked the ceiling of the taxi. Her hat slid down over one ear. Her big suitcase fell over with a bang on the floor and Tom's little suitcase hopped off the seat.

Tom's mother pulled her hat on straight again. Then she looked at her watch. Then she looked out of the window at all the taxis and buses and trucks.

Once more she called to Bill on the front
seat:

"Taxi-driver man, first it's a cop that makes
you stop; then you get stuck behind a truck.
Now the traffic is in our way. We're likely to
sit here the rest of the day. We're *horribly* late
and the train won't wait!"

So Bill began to blow his horn. "Honk!
honk!" shrieked the little taxi. "Honk! honk!
HONK!!!

"We want to go. You make us slow! We're a speedy pair. We want to get there. Honk! *Honk!*

HONK!!!

Honk!

Honk!"

The nearer they came to the station, the more taxis and buses and trucks there were on the street.

Past them all the speedy taxi wiggled and jiggled, twisting and turning and curving and dodging. Tom jounced so hard on the little let-down seat that he could hardly see all the trucks and taxis and wagons and buses on the street.

Suddenly they stopped, and Bill blew the horn again. "Honk!

Honk!

HONK!"

Down the street, up above the station, they
could see the big station clock. In five minutes
the train would go. They really were very, terribly, awfully, horribly late, and they knew the
train wouldn't wait.

Then suddenly, jerk, jerk! The traffic began to move. First a taxi, then a bus, then a truck, then more taxis, more buses, more trucks, till the whole line was moving. The speedy little taxi wiggled through the traffic. It dodged around a bus and it twisted around a truck and it whizzed past a taxi. Tom's mother kept looking at the big station clock. It said four minutes before the train went. Then three minutes. Then two minutes—and the little taxi drew up by the station.

Tom jumped out of the taxi while his mother gave Bill the money. She grabbed her big suitcase. Tom grabbed his little suitcase. And off they ran, thump, thump, thump, thumpety, thumpety, thumpety.

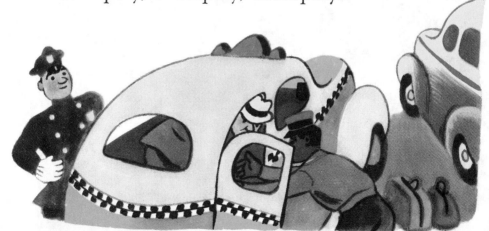

Bill looked after them and grinned at his yellow taxi. "Sure," he said. "We're a speedy pair—we got them there."

And it was true. The conductor was just ready to signal the engineer to start.

But he saw Tom and his mother come running down the platform and he waited for them. He took the big suitcase from Tom's mother, held the door open for her, and handed her the big suitcase. Tom stepped on the train after her, panting from his run and holding his little suitcase.

"All aboard!" called the conductor, waving his hand to the engineer.

Then the conductor swung onto the train just as it began to move. "You're a fast runner," he said to Tom. And to Tom's mother he said, "Lady, you just made it."

Tom was still breathing hard but he managed to gasp out, "We made it—because—we had such a speedy taxi—and speedy driver. You should have seen—that taxi hurry!"